THE OMNIVERSE'S DESTINY

BOOK1 OF *FORGOTTEN ASURA KING TRILOGY*

LAKSHYA SAINI

I DedicateThis Book ToThe Following

> My Parents

> My Elder Brother

> My Teachers

> My Friends

Contents

Chapter 1: A New Life

Raghav had always lived a quiet life in the small, remote village nestled in the mountains of Himachal Pradesh. The village was surrounded by towering peaks, their snow-capped tips barely visible through the mist. The villagers lived simply, their days dictated by the rhythms of nature, the seasons, and the old customs that had been passed down through generations.

Every morning, Raghav would wake up at dawn, the sound of temple bells ringing in the distance. He would offer a prayer to the gods, seeking peace and guidance. The temple was a sacred place, where the villagers came to offer their prayers and sacrifices. It was built from ancient stones, each carved with intricate designs that told stories of long-forgotten gods and demons.

The people in the village were kind, but there was always a feeling of distance between them and Raghav. He didn't quite fit in. He had always felt like there was something more to his life, something beyond the quiet village life he led. Raghav's eyes often wandered to the distant mountains, as if they were calling to him. He could never explain it, but he knew there was something out there, waiting for him.

His mentor, Guru Vishwanath, was an old man who had lived in the village for many years. He was the wisest man

Raghav knew, and it was under his guidance that Raghav had learned the sacred texts and ancient rituals. Guru Vishwanath always spoke of the power within each person, a power that could connect them to the divine. Raghav had spent years trying to understand these teachings, but it was never enough. He could sense there was something more—something beyond what Guru Vishwanath had shared.

As the village prepared for its annual festival, a celebration of the gods and the harvest, Raghav couldn't shake the feeling that this year would be different. The festival was always a time of joy and merrymaking, with songs and dances around the fire. It was the highlight of the year, but for Raghav, it felt like something much more important was about to unfold.

And then, she appeared.

Isha was a newcomer to the village, a young woman with striking features and an air of mystery about her. She had come from a distant city, seeking refuge in the mountains, away from the bustle of modern life. Her beauty was undeniable, but it was her intelligence and kindness that captivated Raghav. There was something about her that drew him in, something he couldn't explain.

At first, their interactions were simple—brief exchanges during the festival, polite smiles shared over meals. But with each passing day, Raghav found himself thinking about her more and more. It was as if their souls had already met in some distant past, and now, fate had brought them together once again.

Isha, too, seemed to sense this connection. She would look at him with a depth that was unsettling, as if she could see into his very soul. Sometimes, when their eyes met, Raghav felt as though she knew him better than anyone else—better than he knew himself.

One evening, as the festival reached its peak, Raghav found himself alone with Isha by the temple steps. The moonlight bathed the village in a soft glow, and the distant sound of drums echoed in the night. Isha spoke first.

"Raghav," she said softly, "There's something different about you. I can sense it."

Raghav's heart skipped a beat. It was as though she had read his mind. He didn't know how to respond, so he simply nodded.

"I feel it too," he replied, his voice barely above a whisper. "There's something... beyond what I understand. It's been with me my whole life."

Isha smiled, a knowing smile, and for the first time, Raghav felt as though he wasn't alone in his confusion. As they sat there, under the stars, a quiet understanding passed between them. But little did Raghav know, this was only the beginning. His life was about to change in ways he could never have imagined.

That night, Raghav had a dream. It wasn't like the other dreams he had often experienced—vivid, strange, and filled with an overwhelming sense of déjà vu. In this dream, he saw himself standing in the middle of a vast battlefield, surrounded by thousands of warriors. His hands were glowing with a powerful energy, and in his grip, he held a weapon unlike anything he had ever seen. It hummed with an unnatural power, and the air around him crackled with raw energy.

He tried to focus, but the dream shifted. The image of a massive throne appeared before him. On it, sat a figure whose eyes burned with an intensity he could not comprehend. The figure looked at him and spoke one word: "Kalki."

Raghav woke up in a cold sweat. The word echoed in his mind, but he didn't understand its meaning. He had heard it before—somewhere, somehow—but where? Who was the figure in his dream? And why did he feel such an overwhelming connection to it?

The next day, as Raghav went about his morning routine, he couldn't shake the feeling that something important had been set in motion. The dream, Isha, the growing sense of confusion—it was all coming together. But he didn't know how.

That evening, as the villagers danced around the fire, celebrating the festival, Raghav found himself alone, staring at the distant mountains. The world felt different somehow. He couldn't explain it, but he knew that his life was no longer his own. He was standing at the edge of something—something vast and unknown.

Little did he know, the festival was the beginning of a journey that would take him far beyond the life he had known, a journey that would awaken powers he didn't understand and force him to confront a past he had long forgotten.

Chapter 2: The Revelation

The days after the festival were unusually quiet. The village returned to its peaceful routine, and the vibrant celebrations of the previous week seemed like a distant memory. Yet, for Raghav, nothing felt ordinary anymore. His thoughts constantly drifted back to his dream—the image of the battlefield, the glowing weapon in his hand, and the mysterious figure who had spoken to him. It was as though the dream was more than just a passing vision; it felt like a message, an invitation to something greater.

Raghav's interactions with Isha also began to change. She no longer felt like just a stranger who had come to the village. There was an unspoken bond between them, a connection that neither of them fully understood but could not ignore. Their conversations were no longer just casual chats; they delved deeper into matters of the soul, the universe, and the ancient teachings that Raghav had learned from Guru Vishwanath. It was as though Isha shared his curiosity about the mysteries of life, and together, they explored the ancient scriptures, seeking answers to questions that had long troubled Raghav's mind.

One afternoon, as the sun began to set behind the mountains, casting long shadows across the village, Isha invited Raghav to meet her by the temple. She had something important to discuss. Raghav felt a mixture of excitement and nervousness as he made his way there, his heart racing in anticipation of what was to come.

When he arrived, Isha was standing at the foot of the temple steps, her face serene as usual, but her eyes gleamed with an intensity that Raghav had not seen before. She motioned for him to sit beside her, and he did so without question. The air around them seemed charged, as if the very atmosphere was waiting for something.

"I've been having dreams," Isha began, her voice low and steady. "Strange dreams, much like yours. But I'm not sure how to interpret them."

Raghav looked at her, startled. Could it be that she, too, was experiencing the same strange visions?

"What kind of dreams?" Raghav asked, leaning in slightly, eager to understand.

"I see images—of destruction, of battles, of great warriors. But the most disturbing part is the figure that appears at the end of each dream. He speaks to me, just as he did to you. His name is Kalki."

The mention of the name sent a chill down Raghav's spine. Kalki—he remembered the word from his own dream. It was the name of a divine incarnation, the future avatar of Vishnu, who was destined to appear during the Kali Yuga, the age of darkness and strife. The thought of such a being entering their world filled Raghav with a mixture of awe and dread.

"Are you saying you've seen this Kalki figure too?" Raghav asked, his voice barely a whisper.

Isha nodded slowly, her eyes distant. "Yes, but there's more. In my dreams, I am told that we have a role to play in this. We are connected to the arrival of Kalki in some way, but I don't know how. I feel as though we have been chosen for something much larger than ourselves."

Raghav's mind raced as he processed her words. Could it be true? Were their destinies intertwined with the arrival of this powerful figure? And if so, what did it mean for them, for their world?

"I've spent years studying the ancient texts, the prophecies, and the teachings of the sages," Isha continued. "There is a line in the Bhagavad Gita that speaks of this time. It says that when darkness prevails and evil grows stronger, a divine being will appear to restore balance to the world."

Raghav's heart skipped a beat. He knew the verse she was referring to. It was one of the most sacred teachings in the Gita, often recited by Guru Vishwanath.

The verse spoke of divine intervention during times of great turmoil—when humanity had lost its way and needed guidance.

Raghav had always believed these words to be a distant ideal, something that spoke of a time far in the future. But now, sitting beside Isha, it seemed as though the prophecy was unfolding before their eyes.

"I think it's time we seek answers," Raghav said, his voice firm with newfound determination. "We need to understand what this means for us and the world around us."

Isha nodded, a look of agreement on her face. "I've been researching this for some time. There are hidden texts, old scrolls in forgotten temples, that speak of the coming of Kalki. We must find them."

The two of them set off together, embarking on a journey that would take them far beyond the quiet village where they had once lived. The answers they sought were hidden in the farthest corners of the world, in places untouched by time and forgotten by most. But as they prepared to leave, a part of Raghav still felt uncertain. Was he truly ready to face what lay ahead? Was he prepared for the truth that would inevitably reveal itself?

As they began their journey, the winds seemed to whisper of danger and darkness. The shadows of the unknown stretched out before them, and Raghav knew that the road ahead would be perilous. Yet, despite the fear, he also felt a strange sense of purpose. The pieces of his life, once scattered and disjointed, were beginning to fall into place. This was the beginning of something much larger than he had ever imagined—a journey that would take him into the heart of the divine and challenge everything he thought he knew about the world

Chapter 3: The Journey Begins

The early morning light filtered through the trees, casting long shadows across the path as Raghav and Isha set out from the village. The air was crisp, and the quiet stillness of the surrounding forest seemed to hum with an unspoken energy. Raghav could feel the weight of the unknown pressing upon him. The path they were about to take was not just a physical journey—it was a journey into the heart of a prophecy, one that would reveal the secrets of the ancient world and the very future of humanity.

"I've heard stories of the hidden texts," Isha said as they walked side by side. Her voice was calm, but there was an undercurrent of excitement. "There are temples deep in the mountains, places where the sages once meditated and wrote the ancient scriptures. These texts contain knowledge that has been lost for centuries, knowledge that may hold the key to understanding Kalki's arrival."

Raghav nodded, though a part of him wondered if they were truly ready for what lay ahead. The journey they had embarked on felt like something out of a legend, and yet, here they were, two ordinary people with no special training or divine powers, seeking answers to questions that had confounded sages and kings for generations.

As they walked, Raghav's mind kept returning to the dream he had, the one with the battlefield and the figure of Kalki. He wondered if he and Isha were meant to play a part in the battle to come, and what their role would be in the grand scheme of things.

After several days of travel, they reached the foot of the mountain where the first temple was said to lie hidden.

The landscape was rugged, the air thin, and the journey ahead would be challenging. But Raghav could not ignore the feeling that they were on the brink of something monumental.

They set up camp near a stream, the sound of rushing water filling the silence. Isha, ever the practical one, began preparing their meal, while Raghav sat near the fire, lost in thought. The stars had begun to appear in the sky, twinkling like tiny diamonds, and the night was growing colder.

"I've been thinking about the verses in the Bhagavad Gita," Raghav said, breaking the silence. "The ones you mentioned earlier. It's hard to fathom the idea of a divine being like Kalki coming to Earth. But if it's true, then what does that mean for us? For the world? Will the darkness really grow so strong that we need a savior?"

Isha looked up from the fire, her gaze thoughtful. "The world is changing. We see it in the way people behave, in the way greed, hatred, and violence have taken hold of so many hearts. The age of Kali Yuga is upon us, and as the Gita says, when dharma falters, the divine incarnates to restore balance. But perhaps it's not just about Kalki alone. Perhaps there is something we must do to prepare the way for his arrival."

Raghav felt a shiver run down his spine. The thought of playing a role in such a cosmic event was both thrilling and terrifying. He had always felt a deep sense of connection to the teachings of the sages, but now, those teachings seemed more real than ever before.

"We need to find the texts," Raghav said resolutely. "The answers must be hidden there."

As the night grew darker, Isha began chanting softly under her breath. Her voice, calm and melodic, seemed to blend with the sounds of the night, creating a sense of peace and grounding in the midst of their uncertainty. Raghav watched her, admiring her grace and inner strength. It was clear to him now that Isha was not just a companion on this journey—she was a guide, a source of wisdom who had been placed on his path for a reason.

The next morning, after a brief rest, they continued their ascent up the mountain. The air grew colder and thinner as they climbed, and the path became more treacherous. Raghav's breath came in short gasps, but his determination pushed him forward. He had no choice but to continue; the answers they sought were somewhere ahead.

As they neared the summit, they came across an ancient stone temple, half-hidden by thick vines and moss. The structure was weathered by time, but its stone pillars still held a sense of majesty, and the carvings along the walls seemed to tell stories of forgotten gods and heroes.

"This must be it," Isha said, her voice a mixture of awe and reverence. "This is the temple where the texts are said to be hidden."

They entered the temple cautiously, the cool stone floors echoing beneath their feet. The air inside was thick with the scent of incense and age, and the faint sound of distant chanting seemed to reverberate off the walls. At the far end of the temple, in a small alcove, they found what they had been searching for: a set of ancient scrolls, their edges worn and brittle with time. The scrolls were covered in strange symbols, and the writing was a mixture of Sanskrit and another, even more ancient script.

"This is it," Raghav whispered, awe-struck by the sight of the scrolls. "This is what we've been looking for."

Isha carefully unrolled the first scroll, her eyes scanning the text. As she read, her expression changed, a flicker of recognition crossing her face.

"These are the teachings of the sages," Isha said, her voice trembling. "They speak of the arrival of Kalki, but they also speak of a prophecy involving two individuals—two souls who will play a pivotal role in his coming. The prophecy is clear: 'When the time comes, the chosen ones will awaken, and the world will be ready for the return of the divine.'"

Raghav felt a surge of energy course through him. The words felt like a confirmation of everything he had felt deep inside—a feeling that he and Isha were not just ordinary travelers, but key players in the unfolding of a divine plan.

"We are the ones," Raghav said, his voice steady with conviction. "We've been chosen to awaken the world to what is coming. The time for Kalki's arrival is near."

Isha nodded, her eyes filled with both awe and fear. "But the path ahead will not be easy. We must prepare ourselves, for the darkness that will arise in this world will test us in ways we cannot yet imagine."

Raghav stood tall, his heart filled with purpose. "We will face whatever comes. Together."

Chapter 4: The Prophecy Unveiled

The wind howled through the temple's broken windows, carrying with it a sense of urgency. Raghav and Isha sat cross-legged before the ancient scrolls, the faint glow of the morning sun casting shadows on the walls around them. The prophecy Isha had uncovered seemed to pulse with a strange energy, as if the very words were alive and waiting for their time to be revealed.

Isha held up another scroll, one that seemed more intricately adorned than the others. The script was written in an even older form of Sanskrit, and the edges of the paper were inscribed with symbols Raghav did not recognize. His mind raced as he wondered what secrets these scrolls held.

"This scroll speaks of the key," Isha said softly, as if unsure whether to speak aloud. "It says that the key to unlocking Kalki's arrival is hidden in the hearts of those who truly understand the ancient truths. The prophecy is not just about a physical savior—it is about the awakening of divine consciousness within us all."

Raghav felt a deep sense of reverence for the words she spoke. It was clear now that the journey they had undertaken was not just one of discovery, but of transformation. They were not only searching for knowledge but for a way to awaken something greater within themselves, something that could connect them to the divine.

"The key," Raghav repeated, his voice a low murmur. "What is the key? Is it something we have to find, or is it something we must become?"

Isha's eyes met his, her gaze steady and unwavering. "It is both. The key lies within you, Raghav. It lies within all of us. We must remember who we truly are, beyond the illusions of this world. When we do, the divine consciousness will reveal itself, and Kalki will come, not as a single savior, but as the collective awakening of humanity."

Raghav's heart began to race. Could it be true? Could the divine consciousness truly awaken within him, within them both? The weight of their journey was suddenly clearer—this was not merely about finding ancient texts or uncovering hidden prophecies. It was about transformation, about becoming something more than what they were.

"We have to prepare ourselves," Raghav said, his voice filled with determination. "We must understand these teachings. The world will not be ready for Kalki until we are ready to receive him."

Isha nodded, the fire in her eyes matching his own. "The world is filled with darkness, and it is growing. People are lost, searching for answers in places that can't offer them hope. But we can be the light. If we awaken ourselves, we can help others awaken too. And together, we will usher in the age of Kalki."

As Raghav looked at the scrolls, he could feel the weight of their message settling into his being. The answers they sought were not just hidden in these ancient texts—they were inside them, inside every human heart. And it was their mission to unlock those answers, to become the living embodiment of the prophecy.

The days that followed were filled with long hours of study and meditation. Raghav and Isha poured over the ancient scrolls, their minds stretching to understand the vastness of the knowledge contained within them. They practiced the teachings with a fervor, immersing themselves in the mantras, the meditation techniques, and the sacred verses that spoke of Kalki's arrival and the restoration of dharma.

But even as they meditated, the world outside seemed to grow more chaotic.

The village they had left behind was no longer a place of peace. News came of unrest in distant lands—of violence, greed, and corruption spreading like wildfire. People were turning on each other, and the darkness that the sages had warned of was creeping into the hearts of many.

One evening, as Raghav sat by the fire, his thoughts turning inward, Isha joined him, her face etched with concern.

"It is happening, Raghav," she said, her voice soft but filled with conviction. "The darkness is spreading faster than we anticipated. People are losing hope, and the world is slipping deeper into chaos. We must act soon. The time is near."

Raghav looked at her, his gaze steady. "We must awaken the key, Isha. We have to make people understand what is coming. They need to see the light."

Isha nodded. "But how do we do that? How do we awaken an entire world?"

Raghav stood up, his eyes fixed on the distant mountains. He felt a surge of energy, a sense of purpose that was beyond anything he had ever known.

"The answer is in the teachings," he said slowly. "We must spread the message of dharma. We must teach people to look beyond the material world, to reconnect with their true selves. Only then can the divine consciousness awaken. Only then can Kalki come."

Isha stood beside him, her hand gently resting on his shoulder. "We will do it together, Raghav. We are not alone in this."

As they stood together, gazing out into the horizon, a sense of calm descended upon them. The journey ahead would not be easy, but they were no longer afraid. They had found their purpose, and they would face whatever came with unwavering faith.

Chapter 5: The First Spark of Change

The journey ahead seemed daunting, but Raghav and Isha felt a growing sense of resolve. They had spent weeks in the temple, absorbed in study and meditation, preparing themselves for the challenge that lay before them. But the world outside was changing too. Darkness, as the scriptures had foretold, was beginning to seep into every corner of the land.

The distant sound of drums echoed through the early morning air, signaling that unrest had reached the borders of their peaceful village. The people had become restless, fearful of the unknown. The winds of war were stirring, and with it came greed, hatred, and fear—forces that threatened to engulf everything.

Raghav and Isha had known that this moment would come. They had been prepared, but it was still difficult to see the change unfold. The villagers were no longer the simple, trusting people they had once known. Fear had taken root in their hearts, and with fear came suspicion and anger.

"We can't wait any longer," Isha said one evening, as they sat before the sacred fire, its flames flickering in the growing darkness. "We have to act now. If we don't show them the way, they will be lost forever."

Raghav nodded. "The time has come to bring the light to those who are ready to see it. We can't force the world to change, but we can guide those who are willing to listen."

Together, they began to travel across the land, sharing the teachings they had uncovered. They went from village to village, from town to town, speaking of dharma, of balance, and of the awakening of divine consciousness. They spoke of Kalki—not as a distant figure to be awaited but as the embodiment of every person's potential to bring about change.

The first spark of change came unexpectedly. It was in a small village, one that had long been plagued by infighting and mistrust. The villagers, driven by fear of their neighbors, had closed themselves off from each other, unwilling to work together. When Raghav and Isha arrived, they found a group of people gathered in the square, arguing over the next course of action. The air was thick with tension, and it seemed impossible to bring them to any common ground.

Raghav stepped forward, his presence commanding attention. "You are not enemies," he said, his voice strong but calm. "You are brothers and sisters, each carrying the same light within you.

You have allowed fear to blind you to your true selves. The only way to overcome the darkness is by coming together in unity."

The crowd fell silent, unsure of what to make of his words. But Isha, with her gentle presence, added, "We are all connected. The divine consciousness flows through each of us, and it is only when we act as one that the light of dharma can shine through."

For a moment, nothing happened. The villagers stared at them, skeptical. But then, something shifted. One of the elders, an old woman whose face had been weathered by years of hardship, stepped forward. She looked at Raghav and Isha, her eyes filled with both sorrow and hope.

"We have forgotten who we are," she whispered. "We have let fear control us, and it has torn us apart. But I can feel it. There is a spark within me, a truth I have long ignored. Perhaps... perhaps it is not too late."

The others looked at her, unsure at first, but then the spark of understanding spread. Slowly, one by one, they began to lower their weapons, to set aside their grievances. The darkness that had held them captive began to recede, and for the first time in years, the villagers spoke to each other with kindness.

That night, as the fire blazed brightly, Raghav and Isha sat with the villagers, sharing food and stories. It was a small victory, but it was a victory nonetheless. The first spark of change had been ignited.

As Raghav and Isha continued their journey, they encountered more villages, more towns, each struggling with its own set of challenges. Some were filled with fear, while others were gripped by greed. But wherever they went, they spoke the same truth—the divine consciousness was within them all, and only by awakening it could they truly find peace.

The message began to spread, slowly but surely. People began to look within themselves, to see beyond the illusions that had clouded their vision. They realized that the change they sought could not be found in the world around them—it had to come from within.

But the darkness was relentless. The forces of corruption, greed, and fear did not give up easily. Raghav and Isha encountered resistance at every turn. Those who had a vested interest in maintaining the status quo fought against the awakening, using every tool at their disposal to keep the people enslaved by their own ignorance.

Still, Raghav and Isha did not falter. They knew that the path ahead would be difficult, but they also knew that they were not alone. The divine consciousness was with them, guiding them every step of the way.

As the days passed, they began to see the fruits of their labor. The small acts of kindness, the shared moments of unity, began to accumulate. A shift was occurring, one that could not be undone. The world was beginning to awaken, and with each step, they drew closer to the arrival of Kalki.

Chapter 6: The Gathering Storm

The winds of change were growing stronger. What had once been a flicker of light, a spark ignited in the hearts of the people, was now turning into a raging fire. As Raghav and Isha journeyed deeper into the lands, they could feel the weight of their mission more intensely with each passing day. The world was at a crossroads, and they were the torchbearers of a transformation that could either save or destroy it.

In every village, the story was the same: people were torn between the desire for peace and the lure of power. Leaders who had once been wise had become blinded by ambition, and the masses, lost in fear, looked for someone to follow. But Raghav and Isha knew that the path forward was not about following another leader—it was about awakening the divine consciousness within each individual.

One afternoon, as they walked through a dense forest, Isha spoke quietly. "I can feel it, Raghav. The darkness is growing stronger. There are whispers in the wind—people are beginning to doubt. They wonder if the divine consciousness can truly overcome the darkness."

Raghav stopped and turned to face her. "Doubt is natural, Isha. It is in the nature of the human mind to question. But we cannot let doubt cloud our purpose. We must continue to show them the way, even if they cannot see it yet. Kalki will come, but only if we are ready."

The path was long, and the land seemed to stretch endlessly before them. Yet, despite the vastness, every corner of the world they visited echoed with the same message—there was unrest, there was fear, and there was a longing for change.

In one particularly troubled town, a young man named Arvind came to them, his eyes filled with both desperation and hope. He had heard their message, and he had seen the changes beginning to take root, but he could not understand why the world seemed to be moving in the opposite direction.

"Why does the darkness still grow, even when we try so hard to awaken the light?" Arvind asked, his voice trembling.

"Why does it seem as though the forces of evil are stronger than ever?"

Raghav and Isha exchanged a look, and Raghav spoke with quiet conviction, "The darkness is a part of this world, Arvind. It is not something we can simply banish with the flick of a finger. It exists because people have forgotten their true nature. But we are not helpless in the face of it. By awakening the divine consciousness within us, we begin to change the world around us."

Isha added, "The world may seem lost, but the power of the divine is in each of us. It is not something external to be found, but something that already exists within. The true battle is not against the world, but against the darkness within our own hearts."

Arvind was silent for a moment, his brow furrowed as he processed their words. "So, you are saying that the world cannot be saved until we save ourselves?"

"Exactly," Raghav replied. "When enough individuals awaken, when enough hearts open, the world will shift. The divine consciousness will illuminate the path for all. Kalki is not a savior to be awaited—it is the potential within us all. We must rise to meet that potential."

Arvind nodded slowly, the weight of the truth settling in. "I understand now," he whispered. "I will do my part. I will awaken the light within me."

As the days passed, Raghav, Isha, and Arvind worked together to spread the message of inner awakening. Arvind became a trusted ally, helping to rally the people and guide them toward a more peaceful existence. But despite their efforts, the forces of darkness were still closing in. The battle between light and shadow was intensifying, and it seemed as though the world was on the brink of collapse.

Raghav knew that the time for waiting was over. "It is time," he said one evening, as the sun dipped below the horizon, casting long shadows across the land. "We cannot delay this any longer. Kalki must rise now, not in the form of a singular being, but in the collective awakening of all humanity."

Isha nodded, her expression calm but resolute. "Let us begin the final journey then. The world is ready."

Chapter 7: The Rising of Kalki

The winds of destiny had shifted. The last vestiges of darkness began to unravel, but the struggle was far from over. As Raghav, Isha, and Arvind gathered their allies, they found themselves on the precipice of a new world, one that had been on the verge of collapse for far too long.

Each village they visited, every town they passed through, echoed with the same deep sorrow—the fear of the unknown and the chaos that followed in the wake of the shifting tides. Yet, there was also an undeniable hope. People had begun to believe in the possibility of change, to see the divine spark within themselves, and to recognize that the world could indeed be different.

But even as this hope grew, so did the opposition. Dark forces, those who thrived in the shadow of fear and chaos, sought to quell the awakening. They understood the power of the divine consciousness and feared its rise. They knew that when humanity truly realized its potential, their reign of control would end. And so, they fought—whispering lies, spreading fear, and nurturing the very darkness that had once held the world in its grip.

Raghav knew that the true battle was no longer one of mere words or influence—it was one of energy. The shift from darkness to light could only occur when enough hearts had fully embraced their true nature and began to awaken the divine within.

On the eve of the final battle, Raghav, Isha, and Arvind stood at the edge of a vast battlefield. The night sky stretched out above them, lit by the pale glow of the moon. The air was thick with tension as the forces of light and darkness prepared to face each other.

"We are not alone in this fight," Raghav said, his voice steady as he looked into the distance. "The divine consciousness flows through all of us. When enough of us awaken, the darkness will not stand a chance."

Isha nodded, her eyes full of determination. "The forces of darkness may seem strong, but they are built on fear, Raghav. Fear is the illusion that weakens them. The light is truth, and truth has the power to cut through any illusion."

Arvind, standing beside them, felt the weight of the moment. His heart pounded in his chest, and he could feel the surge of energy that came with the realization that they were on the brink of something monumental. He had seen firsthand the power of awakening—the transformation it could bring.

"I am ready," he said quietly, his voice resolute. "For the divine. For the light."

And then, as if in response to their words, a great light seemed to pulse across the horizon. It was as though the very stars had awakened, casting their glow across the battlefield.

Raghav raised his hand, and the light around them grew brighter, enveloping them in its warmth. The dark forces began to stir, their forms shifting as they emerged from the shadows, their eyes glowing with malice. But even as they moved forward, a strange unease spread among them. They could feel it—the divine consciousness that was rising within the hearts of all those who had awakened. They could feel the presence of Kalki, not as a single being, but as the collective energy of all who had chosen the path of light.

Raghav closed his eyes and whispered a prayer to the divine. The moment he did, the ground beneath them began to tremble, and a brilliant light shot up into the sky, like a beacon signaling the dawn of a new era.

"It is time," Raghav said, his voice unwavering. "The world is ready."

The battle began.

As the forces of darkness surged forward, they met with an unexpected resistance. The people who had awakened, who had embraced the divine within, stood firm. Their hearts were united, their minds clear, and their resolve stronger than ever.

The light spread like wildfire, reaching every corner of the battlefield. Where once there had been fear, now there was courage. Where once there had been doubt, now there was conviction. And where once there had been darkness, now there was light.

The forces of darkness faltered. They had no power against the truth that was now flowing through the world. They tried to fight, but their strength waned as the light grew brighter, pushing them back into the shadows from which they had emerged.

In the midst of the chaos, Raghav and Isha stood at the center, their eyes glowing with the divine light. They were the conduits through which the awakening flowed, but they knew that they were not alone. The entire world was waking up, and that awakening was the true power.

Arvind, now standing at the front lines, felt the energy surge through him. His body tingled with the divine essence, and his soul soared. He had become one with the divine consciousness, and in that moment, he understood the truth of everything: Kalki had not come in a single form. Kalki was the awakening of all. Kalki was within them all.

As the darkness retreated, the world began to heal. The land that had once been scarred by war and chaos now flourished with life. The people who had once been divided by fear and hatred now stood united in the light.

Chapter 8: The Dawn of a New Era

The victory was not merely a battle won. It was the awakening of a new world, a world where the light of divine consciousness had begun to spread far and wide. The forces of darkness, though powerful, had been overpowered by the truth that had been seeded in the hearts of millions. Now, the world was poised at the edge of a transformation unlike any other in history.

The people of the land were no longer just survivors; they were co-creators of their future. Raghav, Isha, and Arvind knew that the work had only just begun. They had awakened the divine within the hearts of many, but for the world to truly change, that awakening had to spread even further. It was not enough to just push the darkness back—it was essential to nurture the light, to ensure that it grew and flourished in every corner of existence.

The first steps were humble. The cities and towns began to rebuild, not just physically but spiritually. Temples were reconstructed, schools of wisdom established, and communities that had once been divided began to work together in harmony. The teachings of unity, compassion, and the awakening of the divine consciousness spread far and wide, transcending barriers of caste, creed, and race.

Raghav and Isha traveled to distant lands, spreading the message of Kalki—the divine energy that resided within each individual. Everywhere they went, people listened, understood, and began to awaken to their own true potential. Arvind, now fully transformed, took on the role of a teacher and leader, guiding those who had come to realize the power within them. His once uncertain heart now burned with a steadfast clarity of purpose.

And yet, the challenges they faced were not over. The remnants of darkness, although weakened, still lurked in the shadows, trying to resist the flow of light. Fear, doubt, and ignorance still held sway in some parts of the world. There were those who would seek to return to the old ways, the ways of division and conflict.

But the trio knew that their journey was not about defeating darkness once and for all—it was about ensuring that the light continued to grow, that it was nurtured and protected.

As the months passed, Raghav stood on the balcony of a great temple that overlooked the rejuvenated city. The air was crisp with the promise of change, and the people below were alive with activity—children learning, farmers tending to their crops, and families coming together in harmony. It was the dream they had fought for, and it was coming true.

But even in the peace that now reigned, Raghav could sense the undercurrent of challenge. There would always be those who feared the light, those who sought power over others. But he also knew that the world was now different. The divine consciousness had been awakened, and it could not be easily extinguished.

Isha joined him, standing beside him as she gazed down at the city. "This is just the beginning, Raghav," she said softly. "The light is here, but we must continue to nurture it."

Raghav nodded. "Yes, the journey is long. But with every step, we bring the world closer to the truth. The divine consciousness is within us all, and it will guide us forward."

As they stood in silence, a sense of peace settled over them. The world had been healed, and yet, they knew that the healing was a continuous process. It was the flow of life itself—the ebb and rise of light, the constant cycle of awakening.

In the distance, the sun began to rise, casting its golden rays over the land. It was a symbol of the new era, the dawn of a time when humanity would no longer be enslaved by fear, ignorance, or darkness. Instead, they would rise as one, embracing the light within and living in harmony with the divine essence of existence.

Raghav, Isha, and Arvind stood together, knowing that their mission had been fulfilled, but their work would continue for as long as humanity required guidance. They had lit the spark of divinity, and now it was up to the world to nurture it, to grow it, and to carry it forward for generations to come.

Chapter 9: The Shadow of Betrayal

The world that had once been teetering on the brink of annihilation had been restored to peace—yet it was a fragile peace, one that demanded constant vigilance. Isha, Raghav, and Arvind had become the pillars of this new world, symbols of hope and unity. However, beneath the surface of this newfound tranquility, shadows still lurked—dark forces that were waiting for the opportune moment to strike.

Isha had always been the beacon of hope, the one who healed the world with her presence. Raghav was her unwavering protector, and Arvind had stood by them both, a friend and ally. But as the years passed, cracks began to appear. Arvind's once unwavering loyalty began to falter. The whispers of the shadows seeped into his mind, planting seeds of doubt. His heart, once pure, began to harbor resentment and envy, not just of the power that Isha and Raghav wielded, but also the deep love they shared. His desire for control and recognition overshadowed his former ideals.

As tensions simmered, Arvind's internal conflict reached a boiling point. In a moment of overwhelming jealousy and manipulation, he made a fateful decision. He turned against his friends, driven by a dark force that whispered promises of ultimate power. Arvind's betrayal cut deeper than any sword, as he struck at Isha—the one he had once vowed to protect. Her life was extinguished in an instant, and the light of the world dimmed.

The heavens themselves seemed to mourn her death, as the balance of the universe shifted. The loss of Isha was not only a personal tragedy for Raghav but a cosmic one, for she was the embodiment of love and light that held the fabric of the world together.

Chapter 10: The Betrayal

The earth trembled as Raghav discovered the truth—Arvind had struck the fatal blow that ended Isha's life. The shock of this revelation shattered Raghav's heart. He had trusted Arvind like a brother, had fought by his side through countless battles, and had believed in the unity they shared. To learn that it was Arvind, not the devas, who was responsible for Isha's death was a betrayal that ran deeper than any physical wound.

In that moment, Raghav's sorrow transformed into something far more destructive—rage. His love for Isha had been boundless, and her death left a void that could never be filled. But now, that void was consumed by a burning need for vengeance. Raghav's grief was no longer sorrow—it was fury. The light he had once carried in his heart was replaced by the darkness of revenge.

Raghav's cry echoed across the lands, a sound that reverberated through the very fabric of existence. He swore vengeance not only on Arvind but on the devas themselves, blaming them for allowing this tragedy to unfold. He believed that the divine beings had turned a blind eye to his suffering, and he would not rest until the heavens themselves paid for their complacency.

Chapter 11: The Fall into Darkness

Raghav's descent into darkness was rapid and terrifying. No longer was he the noble warrior who had once fought for the light. His transformation was not only physical but spiritual. His once calm demeanor, his sense of justice, and his deep love for Isha all gave way to an insatiable thirst for vengeance.

The world trembled before him as he cast aside all notions of peace and embraced his newfound identity—a demon driven by wrath. His eyes burned with hatred, and his heart was a furnace of fury. His power grew with each passing day, fueled by his grief and rage. The world was no longer a place of hope—it was a battlefield.

The devas, once the guardians of balance and order, were now forced to defend their realm from the wrath of Raghav. Cities fell before his onslaught, and the heavens themselves quaked at the sheer magnitude of his power. Yet, despite their best efforts, the devas were powerless to stop him. Raghav's rage was unyielding.

But in the heart of the cosmos, a force far greater than anything Raghav had ever faced was about to awaken—the Creator, the supreme being who governed the universe. The Creator knew that the world could not survive the destruction that Raghav was sowing, and so, with great care, the Creator prepared to intervene.

Chapter 12: The War with the Gods

As Raghav's power grew, the devas were forced into a desperate battle for survival. Their realm, once a place of peace and balance, now found itself at war with the very force it had once sought to protect. The devas, with all their might, fought against Raghav's unrelenting fury, but it seemed as though they were fighting a losing battle.

The heavens themselves were being torn apart. The skies, once bright and clear, now roiled with dark clouds, a reflection of the chaos that had consumed Raghav's heart. The earth trembled beneath the weight of his rage, and even the stars seemed to flicker in fear.

Yet, in the midst of this cosmic struggle, the Creator took notice. The Creator, who existed beyond the realms of gods and mortals, understood the stakes of this conflict. This was not merely a battle between Raghav and the devas—it was a battle that threatened the very balance of the universe itself.

As the war reached its peak, the Creator made its move.

Chapter 13: The Creator's Intervention

The Creator's arrival was nothing short of divine. In a moment of stillness, the universe seemed to pause, and the cosmos held its breath as the Creator appeared before Raghav. The Creator's presence was overwhelming, an immense and benevolent force that radiated calm.

"Raghav," the Creator said, its voice resonating through every being and every atom, "your anger and hatred have led you down a path of darkness. But even in the depths of your rage, I see the love you once held. This is not your true nature. You were always destined for something greater."

Raghav, consumed by his grief and fury, turned his gaze upon the Creator. "I have lost everything," he said, his voice thick with pain. "My love, my purpose—everything is gone! And you, the gods, you allowed her to die. I will destroy you all."

The Creator's gaze softened. "It was not the devas who killed Isha. It was Arvind, the one you trusted above all others. He is the true enemy, not the divine forces. It was his jealousy, his darkness, that led to Isha's death."

Raghav's heart shattered anew as the truth of Arvind's betrayal sank in. He had been blinded by his grief and rage, and only now could he see the full extent of the treachery that had been committed. Yet, even now, his pain and anger clouded his judgment.

The Creator spoke again, its voice gentle but firm. "You will never bring Isha back, Raghav. But there is something I can offer you. You are not beyond redemption. You must find peace within yourself, only then will the path forward reveal itself."

Chapter 14: The Return of Isha

Raghav's heart was a battlefield, torn between the love he had for Isha and the destructive rage that had consumed him. He kneeled before the Creator, his hands trembling with the weight of his grief and guilt. The Creator's words echoed in his ears, but it was not until he felt the presence of Isha that his soul began to heal.

In the midst of the cosmic chaos, a miracle occurred. The Creator, with a power beyond comprehension, reversed the course of time, undoing the devastation that Raghav had caused. And in that moment, Isha was returned to life.

Raghav felt her presence before he even saw her. The warmth of her love, the light that had once been extinguished, now enveloped him again. The heavens rejoiced, for Isha's return meant that hope, too, had returned. The balance of the universe had been restored.

Tears filled Raghav's eyes as he rose to his feet, his heart swelling with emotions he could barely contain. Isha, the love of his life, stood before him, her gentle smile soothing the torment that had ravaged his soul. For the first time in what felt like an eternity, Raghav felt peace.

"Isha," he whispered, his voice broken, "I thought I had lost you forever."

Isha's smile was tender, filled with compassion and understanding. She stepped forward, her presence radiating warmth. "You have not lost me, Raghav. You never will."

In that moment, the darkness that had consumed him began to recede. The love he shared with Isha was a beacon that pierced through the storm within him. He had walked through hell, but now, with Isha by his side, he understood that true strength was found in forgiveness and love.

Chapter 15: The Creator's Warning

Though Raghav and Isha had been reunited, the Creator's final words carried a heavy weight that neither could ignore. The journey they had walked together had been fraught with pain and loss, yet their journey was far from over.

The Creator's warning was a solemn reminder of the trials yet to come.

"You have endured much, Raghav and Isha," the Creator spoke, its voice filled with both kindness and gravity. "But there is a greater purpose for you both—one that transcends even your love. Your daughter, the child you will one day bear together, will be the reincarnation of the Mother of the Omniverse. She will hold within her a power so vast that it will shape the very fabric of existence itself."

Raghav and Isha exchanged a glance, their hearts filled with both awe and fear. They had known that their love was powerful, but they had never imagined the true extent of what it would bring into the world.

The Creator continued, "When your daughter turns sixteen, a great tragedy will unfold. A challenge will arise that will test the very fabric of existence. The devas, who fear her power, will do whatever it takes to break your bond, to keep her from fulfilling her true purpose. They will stop at nothing to prevent her from coming into her power."

Raghav and Isha stood in stunned silence as the Creator's words sank in. The future was uncertain, and the weight of the responsibility they now carried felt heavier than any burden they had ever known. But the Creator's final words gave them hope:

"Your love, Raghav and Isha, will be the key to her strength. In your love, you will find the courage to face the challenges yet to come. No matter what trials you endure, know this: you will always have each other. And in that love, you will find the power to protect your daughter and ensure that her destiny is fulfilled."

The Creator's form began to fade, and with its departure, the calm that had descended upon the world seemed to

lift, leaving Raghav and Isha to
contemplate the path that lay ahead.
They were no longer just guardians of
each other, but of something far
greater—the future of the entire
universe.

As they turned to return to the mortal
world, the Creator's final warning
lingered in their hearts, a reminder that
their journey was not over, and that the
greatest challenge was yet to come.

To be continued..........